Rise Up!
SPEAK UP!
thank you, i hope
this work brings
you joy!
♡ Tiffany

ISBN 13: 978-1-63489-593-4

Library of Congress Catalog Number has been applied for.
Printed in the United States of America
First Printing: 2023
27   26   25   24   23   5   4   3   2   1

Illustrations by Tiffany Baker
Design by Cindy Samargia Laun

Wise Ink Creative Publishing
807 Broadway St. NE, Suite 46
Minneapolis, MN 55413
wiseink.com

Credit for Assata Shakur's chant:
Shakur, Assata. "To My People By Assata Shakur (written while in prison)".
Articles/letters. 4 July 1973. http://www.assatashakur.org/mypeople.htm

This Book Belongs To

Baby Joy loved living in the big city.

Every morning she woke up to the screech of the bus picking up and dropping off her neighbors. Most mornings, Mama made her favorite—brown sugar oatmeal with apples and peaches.

Auntie's house!

Baby Joy could walk on her own, but she loved riding in her stroller. She would put on the pink sunglasses that her big sister Kennedy gave her. Then Mama and Daddy would push her all through the city.

She loved looking skyward at the tall buildings. She waved hello to her friends on the way to Mama's job, or to Auntie's house, or to community meetings.

Most of all, Baby Joy
loved taking long walks
with her mom around
the giant park.

She watched the birds play in the grass, chirping happily as they found bread crumbs and bits of food that people left behind.

One day, as Baby Joy lay daydreaming, she heard voices and drumming drawing near.
As the crowd came closer, she heard people shout different words, like "freedom" and "justice."

Curious, she asked her mom,
"What's that sound?
Why are they so loud?"

Baby Joy's mom replied,
"There's a protest going on."

"What's a protest, Mama?"
Baby Joy asked.

"A protest is a way for people to speak up when they care a lot about something. Many people speaking up together are more powerful than just one person."

"What are those people speaking up about?" Joy asked.

IS THIS WHY WE PRACTICE OUR FREEDOM CHANT?

"Well, some people here are treated differently than others because of the color of their skin. That isn't fair, and the protesters are using their voices to speak out against it."

BLACK LIVES MATTER
NO JUSTICE NO PEACE
BLM
HANDS UP! DONT SHOOT
SAY THEIR NAMES
LIVES MATTER
NO ICE NO PEACE

The voices of the protesters
grew louder and closer to them.
Baby Joy suddenly felt afraid.

"Are they going to hurt us, Mama?"

"No, Baby Joy. They are
calling us over to join them."

She felt excited now. She could see people she knew in the crowd. Her big sisters Kennedy and Jayda and her big brother PJ waved and smiled as they chanted,

"All power to the people!"

"Can we join the protest, Mama? Pretty, pretty please?"

"Yes, we can, and we should."

As they walked toward the protest, Mama's friend brought them a large sign.

Mama showed it to Joy and said,
"This side says *End police violence*, and the other side says *We want justice!*"

Baby Joy and Mama joined the crowd. Joy chanted with the people around her. Mama and Daddy had taught her chants at home, but it felt good to shout them out loud with others.

"Mama, what does that one say?" she asked, pointing to it.

"It says, *Black Lives Matter*."

"What do we want?
Justice!

When do we want it?
Now!"

"NO JUSTICE,
NO PEACE!"
they shouted
in unison.

The protesters marched
through the streets of
their city. Baby Joy felt
their powerful energy.
She wriggled with
excitement and glee, and
she smiled at everyone
who passed her way.

She saw friends who were little like her and others who were much bigger but excited just like her. Her friend Rocky held up a baby bullhorn. Genesis sat on her dad's shoulders so she could see everything.

RISE UP!

Other kids held high the signs they had made with markers and crayons.
Her favorite sign was painted with bright reds, bold blues, and beautiful purples.

The longer they walked, the more people joined.
"NO JUSTICE, NO PEACE!" they shouted proudly.

A bundle of white balloons rose into the sky as the people shouted the names she had heard Mama and Daddy talk about at home.

"These are names we never want to forget, Joy," Mama told her. "Their lives matter, and we say their names to remember why protesting for our freedom is so important."

Joy heard their voices rising with the balloons, higher than the tallest buildings downtown. She imagined everyone in her city hearing them. Joy felt powerful.

"Mama, can we shout
Assata Shakur's chant?
That one is my favorite."

"We sure can!"
Mama answered.

Joy couldn't wait. She
jumped out of her stroller,
and Mama held her in her
arms as they chanted.

"We have a duty to fight for our freedom! We have a duty to win!"

When the bright sky grew dark, the protest ended. The crowd grew smaller and smaller. As they walked home, Baby Joy felt excited but also very tired. She knew that she had been a part of something special.

At home, Baby Joy walked over to her alphabet toys in a pile on the floor. She knelt down and picked up the letter *J*, just as she had seen on her mom's sign.

"Look, Mama!" she exclaimed.
"*J* is for Justice!" Her mom smiled
from ear to ear.

"You're absolutely right, Baby Joy.
We need more justice in the world . . .
and a lot more joy."

"J is for Justice!"

USE YOUR VOICE TO SPEAK OUT AGAINST INJUSTICE

- Learn about social justice issues by reading, doing research, and asking questions of a trusted adult.

- Ask questions in class and do your best to listen.

- Once you understand what is happening, you can discuss the issue with your peers and/or a trusted adult.

- Attend a meeting with a trusted adult.

- Write a story, a poem, or a rap, or paint to express how you feel and/or to educate others.

- Find the courage to use your voice. Even if your voice shakes, challenge yourself to speak up.

- Get involved at your own pace and do your best to get out of your comfort zone.

- Continue to practice at your own pace. Rest, reflect, and repeat.

- Thank your volunteers and supporters and give yourself a giant hug.

ORGANIZE YOUR OWN EVENT!
Organize an event to draw people together who might want to learn about the issue. Ask for help from trusted adults, friends, and family members. Think of a name for your event that focuses on the topic. Also, think about the outcome you want to see. When will the event be held, and for how long? Where will the event be? Decide who the audience is and who will lead the discussion. Create a checklist of things to do with your volunteers and decide who will do each task on the list.

GLOSSARY

Activist: One who advocates for change on one or more issues and is willing to accept any risks or consequences that come along with speaking truth to power.

Advocate: Someone who stands up for the rights of others, especially those who are being treated unfairly. One who champions a cause or causes that are important.

Chant: Powerful words spoken or repeated in a rhythmic way, typically at a protest, march, or rally.

Empathy: The act of having genuine, heartfelt compassion for the plight of others who experience harm, abuse, or difficulty.

Equality: Fair and just treatment of all people, regardless of our differences.

Freedom of speech: Our right under the U.S. Constitution to speak up and speak out about what we believe.

Justice: Treating others with fairness in society and under the law.

Police brutality: Unjust physical abuse and/or assault at the hands of police. Could also include the use of physical and chemical weapons or unjust treatment and arrest.

Protest: Gathering together to stand for or against something that is having an impact on community members or on society as a whole.

Racism: Prejudice plus power; when those in a dominant racial group consciously or subconsciously use power and privilege to oppress and/or harm others.

CHANTS FOR KIDS

What do we want?
Justice!
When do we want it?
Now!

—

Whose streets?
Our streets!
Whose land?
Native land!

1, 2, 3
Stop police brutality!

—

When Black lives are
under attack,
what do we do?
Stand up, fight back!

No more lies.
No more hate.
Diversity makes
America great!

—

I may be young,
but this I know
We must change
the status quo!

NEKIMA'S YOUNG ACTIVISTS

Ade Williams
Anakin Rodriguez
Assata Joy Armstrong
Braelyn Johnson
Cairo Camille Quinn Johnson
Cali Williams
Derek Antonio Beevas, IV
Gabriel Leggett
Genesis Irene Beevas
Jasir Malik Alexander Turner
Lionel Jackman Brickwedde
Loyalty Armstrong
Michaela Donaldson
Oaklynn Donaldson
Olivia Peterson
Rocky Buckanaga Williams
Ryland Westerlund
Tahj Kingston Key'Shon Dinkins
Talib Williams
Taurus Williams
Yara Williams
Zaire Demetrius Zay'Veon Dinkins
Zara Jackman

ABOUT THE AUTHOR

"When we have young folks who demand their rights and challenge adults to get uncomfortable—that is how we will move to a better world."

NEKIMA LEVY ARMSTRONG is an award-winning civil rights lawyer, activist, and former president of the Minneapolis NAACP. She is a frequent speaker on national news outlets about racial justice advocacy and public policy, most notably including an interview with Oprah. Her work includes founding the Racial Justice Network, an executive director role at the Wayfinder Foundation, and formerly serving as a tenured professor of law at the University of St. Thomas. Nekima regularly organizes protests in Minneapolis—attending with her daughter, Assata Joy, who loves chanting and marching with her community. She grew up in Jackson, MS, and South Central Los Angeles.

For racial justice resources and information on speaking engagements, visit NekimaLevyArmstrong.com.

ABOUT THE ILLUSTRATOR

"My desire is to express emotionally powerful artwork in which people witness a complex reflection of themselves."

TIFFANY BAKER is a Chicago-born, Brooklyn-based visual artist working in oil, acrylic, graphite, digital, and glass. Tiffany's artistic style of realist portraiture is marked by vibrant palettes and considered attention to her subject's grooming. Tiffany has created illustrations for *Good Night Stories for Rebel Girls: 100 Real-Life Tales of Black Girl Magic*, The HBO adaptation of Ta-Nehisi Coates's novel *Between the World and Me*, CNN, and VH1's *Black Girl Beauty*. Tiffany creates murals in her local neighborhood of Bed-Stuy on community refrigerators for mutual aid initiatives aimed at fighting food insecurity. Tiffany holds a Bachelor of Industrial Design from Pratt Institute and has trained at SVA and the New York Academy of Art.

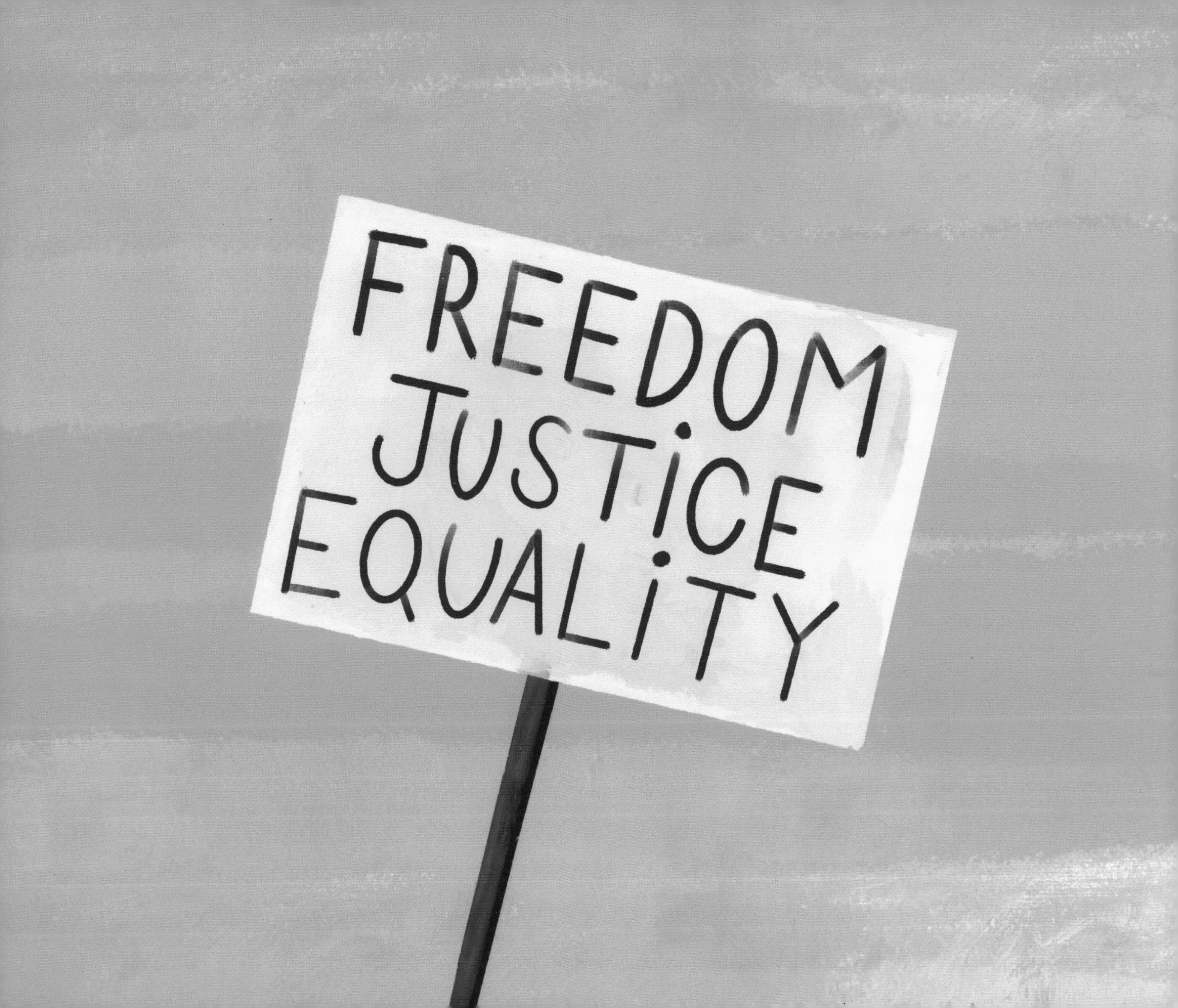
FREEDOM
JUSTICE
EQUALITY